Disney WRECK-IT RALPH

High Score!

Adapted by Cynthia Hands
Illustrated by the Disney Storybook Artists

A GOLDEN BOOK • NEW YORK

ISBN: 978-0-7364-2956-6

randomhouse.com/kids

CRAYONS MANUFACTURED IN CHINA

Book printed in the United States of America

10 9 8 7 6 5 4

Wreck-It Ralph is the Bad Guy in a video game called *Fix-It Felix Jr.*

Wrecking Niceland is what Ralph does best.
But being a Bad Guy is a lonely, thankless job.

Fix-It Felix is the Good Guy in Niceland.
He can fix anything with his magic hammer!

Everyone likes Felix!

Ralph always ends up in the mud.

In Game Central Station, Surge Protector
guards the gate of each video game.

Ralph likes to help anyone in need.
He really is a nice Bad Guy.

Ralph smashes a cake because he wasn't invited to Felix's party!

Ralph has a soda with one of the
soldiers from the game *Hero's Duty*.
He finds out about the Medal of Heroes.

Ralph sneaks into the *Hero's Duty*
game to win the Medal of Heroes!

Sergeant Calhoun is the fearless leader in *Hero's Duty*. Her mission is to defeat all cy-bugs.

The cy-bugs transform into the weapons and machines they eat!

Ralph gets the Medal of Heroes.
The General congratulates him.

Ralph can't get the baby cy-bug off!

Calhoun and Felix team up to find
Ralph and the escaped cy-bug.

In the game *Sugar Rush*, Ralph loses his medal,
and the cy-bug sinks into a pool of taffy.

A girl named Vanellope von Schweetz
takes Ralph's medal!

Vanellope plans to use Ralph's medal
to enter the Random Roster Race.

King Candy, the ruler of *Sugar Rush*, and his assistant, Sour Bill, are ready for the race.

Taffyta, Minty, and Rancis have
their gold coins ready!

Vanellope's kart may be rickety and small, but nothing is going to stop her from racing!

The Donut Police carry out all
of King Candy's orders.

Taffyta tells Vanellope she
is not allowed to race.

Ralph agrees to help Vanellope build a new kart,
and she says she'll win him back his medal!

Felix and Calhoun arrive in *Sugar Rush*
and continue the search for Ralph.

Calhoun and Felix make a great team!

At the kart bakery, Ralph uses his fists to mix the batter for Vanellope's new kart.

The new kart is a little messy,
but Vanellope thinks it's perfect!

Vanellope wants to race, but there's one problem: she doesn't know how to drive!

Ralph builds a racetrack so Vanellope can learn how to drive her kart.

Felix looks for Ralph at King Candy's castle and ends up in the dungeon.

King Candy returns the Medal of Heroes.
He tells Ralph that Vanellope can't race.
If she does, the game will break!

Vanellope thanks Ralph for his help by giving him a homemade medal. He's her hero!

Ralph feels terrible, but he knows
he must destroy Vanellope's kart.

Ralph finds out that King Candy lied to him.
Vanellope *does* belong in *Sugar Rush*!

Ralph asks Felix to fix Vanellope's kart.

Vanellope is a great racer. She
catches up to King Candy in no time!

King Candy turns out to be Turbo, a character from an old racing game who took over *Sugar Rush*.

Vanellope zips toward the finish line! But before she reaches it, the cy-bugs attack!

Calhoun and Felix team up again to
help the residents of *Sugar Rush*!

A cy-bug bites Turbo—and turns him
into a Turbo-bug! Watch out, Ralph!

When Diet Cola Mountain erupts, Turbo-bug
gets zapped! *Sugar Rush* is saved!

Ralph pushes Vanellope across the finish line.

The game resets, and Vanellope
transforms into a princess.

Ralph doesn't need a medal to be a Good Guy. He has the coolest friend in the world to prove it!

Back in his own game, Ralph becomes everyone's favorite Bad Guy!